BIGGEST LITTLE TRUCKSTOP

STARWOOD CHRONICLES, BOOK ONE-CLEAN, SWEET SMALL TOWN ROMANCE

BOBBY HUTCHINSON

SUNFLOWER PUBLISHING

FOREWORD

Dear Reader,

I was born and grew up in this small Rocky Mountain coal mining town of Sparwood, B.C., Canada. Our big claim to fame is THE BIG TRUCK, advertised as the world's largest. I always wanted to start a restaurant near it and call it the Biggest Little Truckstop In The World.

Well, we all know what the failure rate is with restaurants, so instead I decided to write a short romance about an imaginary restaurant called Truckstop, located in Sparwood's imaginary alter ego—the town of Starwood. The other books in the series are:

EVERY LITTLE THING
BIGGEST LITTLE MUSTACHE
And coming soon: BIGGEST LITTLE HEART

I thought you might like a free book, one of another series about doctors and hospitals, life and death—and, of course, love. You can get it here:

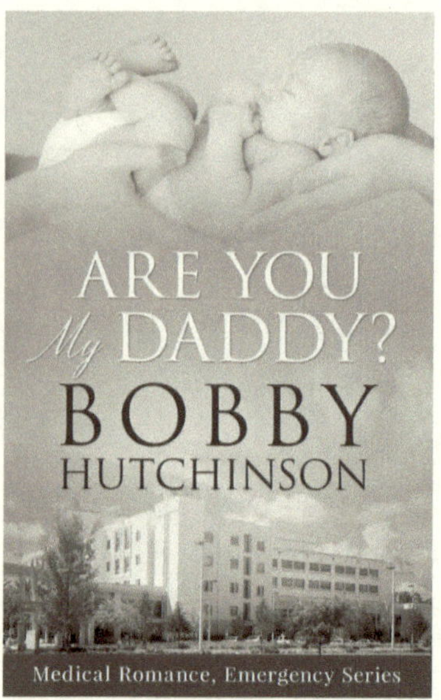

ARE YOU
My DADDY?
BOBBY
HUTCHINSON
Medical Romance, Emergency Series

1

———

"What'll it be?" Mac Ferguson wiped his big hands on his cook's apron and scowled down at the woman in the booth. Three minutes after nine on a sunny June morning and already his day was shot to hell.

He'd been fourteen minutes late getting to work because one of the cows got out, and then when he got here one of the clocks had stopped.

And the bank had just called. They'd refused his application for another loan on the Truckstop. Not enough business income.

Which meant he was going to have to declare bankruptcy and shut the doors on the place, admit defeat once and for all. Anger and frustration made his gut burn. Maybe he was getting an ulcer.

"I know it's not on the menu, but could you please make Susie a smoothie?" The young woman looked up at him, and the little girl beside her did as well.

They both had big green eyes and dark curly hair. The woman had glasses perched on her nose. They both looked pale and tired. The kid was wearing little pink cowboy boots, her mother a pair of well-worn brown ones.

From the kitchen he'd heard them clomping across the wooden floor when they came into the empty cafe a few moments ago. They weren't from Starwood, he knew everyone in town.

The woman had on black tights and some kind of short dress that looked like it was made from one of his mother's bright flowered tablecloths. The kid was in blue jeans and a pink top.

"If it's not on the menu, I don't make it," he said in a curt tone, pointing to one of the many signs on the wall.

"*No substitutions, no special orders,*" it read.

Why the hell did Angie have to get sick and leave him waiting on customers as well as doing the cooking? She knew how hard it was for him, she knew he hated dealing with people, he wasn't good at it. When he'd taken over the Truckstop from his mother, Angie had promised that as long as he cooked, she'd do the people part.

His cousin Angie wasn't exactly Miss Congeniality either, but the regular customers were used to her. And why couldn't his sister come in and give him a hand? Since when was a sick cat more important than helping out her brother?

But that was a ridiculous question. Edna had always put her pets first. Pets over people, you'd think he'd know that. She'd been born when he was four, thirty years ago now, and she'd been nuts over animals ever since she could roll over and smile at the dog.

He and Edna were always called the weirdo Ferguson kids.

"No substitutions," he repeated. "No substitutions, it says so on the sign."

"I know," The woman said. "I did notice that sign and I

wouldn't ask for myself," the woman said in a tremulous, husky voice, shoving her glasses up her nose with her fore-finger. "But Susie's had the flu, and the only thing she'll swallow is a smoothie. If you have a blender, just toss in a banana and some milk. I've got some protein powder in my purse."

He opened his mouth to refuse, but the little girl looked up at him through long dark lashes and said in a tiny voice, "My tummy's really sore and our car got broke and I threw up on Jingles and now he smells bad." Tears welled up in her eyes and her chin trembled. "Mummy has to find a laun-domite and wash him."

"Laund*romat*," the woman corrected automatically, smoothing down the kid's curls.

"Okay, okay." Mac went against his every rule. He hurried into the kitchen, threw a banana and milk into the blender, flipped the switch on high. He was a sucker for kids, and the little girl made him think of the family he'd thought he and Brianna would have together. Plain foolish of him.

Three months ago Brianna had run off with an insur-ance salesman just before they were going to get married. She'd said she just couldn't put up with him anymore. "You're a *screwball*, Mac. I need somebody normal," she'd hollered at him when he asked her why she was leaving.

That had been the beginning of a downward spiral that hadn't slowed since, a lot of it caused by the fact that Brianna had closed out their joint accounts, transferring most of the substantial line of credit to the savings account and then taking it all out as cash.

Sammy, the bank manager, had tried to tell Mac not to give her total signing authority on all his accounts, but they were getting married, right? And to him, marriage was all about trust. His mom and dad had always shared everything. That's what marriage was to him, trust.

Well, he'd been stupid and he was paying for it big time. As always, business was slow, and now he was two months behind on the substantial loan he'd taken out a year ago for the new roof, the new commercial equipment, stove, fridge and dishwasher. The bank had used his savings as security, and now they were gone.

He poured the mix into an ice-cold milkshake container and went back out to the booth, setting the smoothie and a glass in front of the kid. "There you go, missy." He turned to the woman who was typing out a text on her phone. "You want coffee?"

"Yes, please. And thank you so much for making this for her." She dug in her battered handbag and pulled out a plastic bag of green powder, stirring it into the smoothie.

Mac thought it looked disgusting, but the kid didn't seem to mind. "No sweat." He retrieved the coffee pot from the serving station and poured it into her cup. "You want anything else?"

"Maybe some scrambled eggs? And whole wheat toast, please?"

"Number six on the menu, with bacon."

"That'll be good.'

He headed back to the kitchen and made up the order, then plopped the plate down in front of the woman.

"That be all?"

When she nodded, he scribbled out a bill and set it down on the table. He charged her only for number six. There was something about those tiny worn cowboy boots and the battered purse that made him think maybe the two of them might not have much money. And besides, he had no idea what to charge for a smoothie.

"Do you—are you familiar with the mechanic at the garage over there?" She shoved her glasses up and pointed out the window at the Esso. "Is he—is he reliable?"

Mac nodded. "Gilbert's okay." He didn't add that Mac's cousin Floyd, who'd taken over the franchise, was liable to overcharge for whatever Gilbert repaired. Floyd overcharged for everything.

"What's wrong with your ride?"

"I don't know," the woman said. "The car started making this really bad noise just out by the sign that says "Starwood, Home Of The World's Biggest Truck," and then it jerked and stopped and wouldn't start again. Lucky I had CAA, I called and they sent a tow truck right away."

The little girl had been sipping her smoothie, but now she looked up at him. "We saw the World's Biggest Truck, it's called the tiger and it's scary."

"Titan, sweetie. It's called the Titan."

"Oh yeah? It's scary, why's that?" He'd been scared of lots of things when he was little. He still was, bankruptcy being top of the list.

"It looks like it would eat me."

He had to smile at that. From a little kid's viewpoint, the monster truck would look scary. "So no big trucks where you come from, huh?"

She shook her head, making her dark curls bounce. "Nope. No big mountains like here. We used to live in Calvary in Alberta," she volunteered. "But now we're going to Vancouber in B.C, where there's this big lake called an ocean. Mommy's getting a job in Vancouber, right, Mommy?"

"*Calgary*, Susie. And *Vancouver*." She added in an undertone, "And I sure hope I'm getting a job." She glanced around the empty cafe. "I guess you wouldn't need any help around here, mister——?"

She waited, and when he didn't reply she said, "Oh, I'm so sorry. I didn't even introduce myself. My name is Kate. Kate Quigley. This is my daughter, Susanne." She paused. "And you are—?"

"Mac. Mac Ferguson." He wasn't used to having to introduce himself to customers. He mostly stayed in the kitchen, and anyway the town's residents knew him.

In this Canadian Rocky Mountain small town, most everyone knew most everything about most everybody local. And he'd lived in Starwood all of his life, apart from attending trade school. He'd thought of moving somewhere else, but where would he go? They were used to him here. He might be a weirdo, but everyone here knew that. Somewhere else they'd have to find it out all over again.

Any thoughts he'd had about somewhere else had been cut short when his dad died and his mom started losing it. She couldn't manage the farm and all the animals by herself, and she certainly couldn't run the Truckstop. So now he was doing both.

"How do you do, Mr. Ferguson?" Kate held out her hand and he hesitated, then wiped his on his apron before he took it. Her skin was soft, but there were callouses on her palm. He had to wonder what had put them there. Not quite beautiful, Kate Quigley, but she had a killer smile.

Not that he was ever going to get mixed up with a woman again.

"Mac," he repeated. "Everyone just calls me Mac."

"And I'm Kate," she said. She drew in a deep breath and he could tell she was nervous. "Mac, the mechanic said it would take a few days to fix my car because he'd have to order in some parts and they wouldn't be in until the end of the week. He said I could probably get a room over at the hotel, but I checked and it's way over my budget. We're sort of in a bind and I thought maybe.....I'm a real good worker. I did advertising for a gas company in Calgary, but when the price of oil tumbled, the company went bankrupt. Could you maybe ask the boss if I could help out?"

"I am the boss. You ever waitressed before?"

She hesitated and then reluctantly shook her head. "No, but I learn fast. And I'm really good with people."

She must have noticed that he wasn't. "It takes more than a couple days to figure out waitressing." He looked back at the little girl and then at Kate. "And where would she be while you were learning to be a waitress?" He didn't mean it to sound so patronizing.

Now she sounded timid. "Maybe...maybe she could just sit somewhere out of the way and colour or play with her toy horses? She's a really good girl."

The cafe door opened and four of the regulars ambled in, taking their usual booth just behind Kate and the kid.

Mac used their arrival to avoid telling her he wasn't about to hire her. He watched the men to see if they'd abide by his sign that said, *"Take off your hat."*

They did and he nodded to Scooter, ignoring the other three. Scooter had always been half civil to him, not like the others.

"You all want the usual?" Their orders never varied.

"How come Angie's not here?" Floyd, Mac's cousin who now owned the garage, was a crude and rude loudmouth. "You look pretty hot in that apron, Mac. But you ain't got the tits to carry it off. Angie, now, she's got the killer bazooms, right, Sparks? You been there, man, you oughta know, right?"

Sparks snickered, but he sobered quickly when Mac

gave him a venomous look before turning his attention to Floyd. "Watch your mouth, Rudrum," Mac growled, leaning in close and getting right in Floyd's face. "There's a lady and a kid here, in case you haven't noticed. Either keep it clean or get out." He pointed to the sign that said, *"No bad language."*

"I wasn't swearin, I was just statin' facts," Floyd sneered. "And we'd like to go somewhere's else, right, boys?" Floyd looked at his sycophants and they all nodded like puppets. "We'd be happy to go somewhere's else if there was any other greasy spoon in this one horse town. But you got the market cornered, cuz, so you're stuck with us, lucky you." Floyd pretended to laugh, but Mac could see the meanness in his hooded eyes. "So go make us the usual, Ferguson. And I want more cheese on that omelet than I had the other day. Must be economizing, cutting down on cheese, waitressing yourself. Business falling off? But then I don't guess it ever had far to fall." He guffawed again.

Mac ignored him, pouring coffee for the men, carefully setting up a new pot to brew before he went into the kitchen. You had to stay ahead of things.

He swiftly put the four orders together, listening to their ribald conversation while keeping an eye on the clocks. There was plenty of innuendo, but no outright lewdness. *No swearing, the sign said no swearing.*

Fourteen minutes to put the food together. Mac loaded the plates on his arms and pushed through the swinging half doors.

"Anything else?" He smacked their orders down and poured fresh coffee, noticing that instead of leaving, Kate had moved to the far end of the room and was settling Susie to colouring with the crayons and colouring books Angie kept on the front counter.

Mac scribbled out separate bills for Floyd and his posse.

Two couples had come in, settling themselves in the large half rounded booth by the window. Mac was heading over to take their order when Kate intercepted him.

"Let me just try doing this, please?" Her voice was soft, pitched so that only he could hear it. There was a note of desperation there and it made him uncomfortable to have her standing so close to him. She smelled like vanilla.

"Just let me try for an hour or two, you don't have to pay me anything. I can see that running the front as well as doing the cooking is nearly impossible. And if I could learn to waitress I could maybe get a job. In Vancouver. I could help, honest. I don't expect to get paid."

She was right about how difficult it was waiting on people and cooking as well. What the hell. And one off colour remark from Floyd would send her running anyway. Maybe she needed to learn the hard way that waitressing was tough, dirty work.

"Okay, okay. There's clean aprons in the drawer by the window in the kitchen. You need an order pad, number the booths in your head so if we get busy you know where you're at."

As if.

"Then write everything down and number the orders clockwise so you know what belongs to who. And remember, no substitutions." He dug a fresh order pad out from under the counter and handed it to her with a pen, ignoring the jolt of awareness that flickered when their hands touched.

No more women. "Use one of the grey tubs in the kitchen to clear the tables. Do you have any idea how to run the till or use a debit machine?" He knew he sounded grumpy. He hated being attracted to her.

She nodded. "I worked as a cashier for a while when I was in college."

"Good." Even if it was only very temporary, Mac felt a sense of relief as he retreated to the kitchen. She could rob the till, but what the hell. There was only a basic float in it, there hadn't been many customers this morning. And what was one more loss to a sinking ship?

Ten twenty-seven.

In four minutes twenty seconds she appeared at the pass through, reading from her order pad.

"They want whole wheat pancakes with fried eggs, a veggie omelet, waffles and bacon and eggs sunny side up, please."

Mac shook his head. "You've gotta learn to order properly," he barked. "Each order separate. You order by the numbers on the menu. Just write the orders clearly on the pad clockwise and numbered and hand them in to me. Your pad has a carbon, you use your copy for making out the check. If there's four orders I need four chits."

"Okay, got it. Thanks." She leaned on the pass thru and carefully re-wrote what the customers wanted, but Mac was already busy at the stove.

"I know what they want, they're in for breakfast every Tuesday. They golf together. Go pour their coffee."

They were also rumoured to swap partners. Angie had told him. Her daughter's friend's boyfriend's sister claimed to have witnessed the swap. There were few secrets in a town as small as Starwood, but there were also a lot of unsubstantiated rumours. Like the one that he had brain damage.

He shook his head in disgust, moving with a practiced rhythm that didn't need his full attention. He knew by heart the exact recipes for everything. He wanted to put his earphones on to block out the noise of conversation, but he was wary of Floyd and his posse. He needed to listen to what they were up to.

Within sixteen minutes he had the orders up on the pass thru.

Kate carefully and slowly took the orders two at a time over to the table.

Mac watched and shook his head. She needed to learn how to carry four plates a time or the food would be cold before the customers ever got it. He had to admit she was better at the personal stuff than he was though.

She smiled and chatted easily with the golf group, and they were obviously charmed by her. Especially the men. Mac scowled at the old idiots trying to outdo one another at being funny and sexy, each of them sneaking glances at Kate's back-end when she bent to pick up a dropped napkin.

He had to admit it was a very nice rear end. She was tall and really slim, but she had curves in all the right places. A nice round bottom.

Not that he was interested, he reminded himself. He was off women for life. What to do about his healthy sex drive was something he hadn't quite figured out yet. And there was the sadness and sense of loss whenever he thought of Brianna. He'd tried hard for normal around her.

"Hey sweet cheeks, how about a little service over here? Or is old Mac giving it away this morning?" Floyd and his gang were waving their checks in the air.

Mac started out to deal with them but heavy banging on the back door distracted him. It was the dairy delivery and they'd shorted him on coffee cream.

By the time he could break free, loud laughter and Floyd's gravelly voice sounded from the booth. Mac walked over to the pass thru.

"Where'd old Mac find you, honeybun?" Floyd slowly licked his lips, leering up at Kate.

She handed him the portable debit machine and he grabbed her wrist, holding on as she tried to pull away.

"With an ass like that, you need a real man to show you a good time, baby." He stuck out his tongue and waggled it back and forth, getting to his feet, standing as close to her as he could get. "What time you getting off? I could make that a lot more fun, the getting off part."

"Let—go—of—me." She tried to pull away again but Floyd hung on.

Swearing under his breath, Mac slammed through the swinging doors and headed towards them, but before he got there Kate had dropped the debit machine, brought her elbow up sideways, breaking Floyd's grip and then using both fists to punch him hard right in the gut in a lightning fast one two combo. The co-ordinated series of moves were well executed.

Floyd let out a loud "oomph" and doubled over just in time for Mac to grab him by the back of his belt and his shirt collar and frog march him to the door, yanking it open and shoving the other man out on the sidewalk.

"Don't come back," he warned. "You're not welcome here ever again." Mac slammed the door shut and turned towards the other three men.

"You guys got any issue with that?" He glared at one after the other.

They all shook their heads, not looking at him. They were staring at Kate.

2

———

She'd reacted automatically. Umi, her self-defence teacher, would have been proud.

And she'd just blown any chance at this job. Kate picked up the debit machine from the floor, doing her best to hide the adrenaline tremors that were making her tremble and walked back over to the table.

First the one called Sparks and then the other two held out their credit cards. They looked stunned as she ran them through. She was pitifully grateful that the debit machine hadn't broken when it hit the floor. How would she ever have paid for *that*?

The men got warily to their feet, shooting sideways glances at Mac, edging carefully past her. They lost no time leaving.

When the door closed behind them, she let out the breath she'd been holding.

"I'm so sorry." She looked up at Mac. "I thought I'd last longer than an hour at this. But thanks for giving me a chance." She turned away and untied her apron before he could see the tears that were blurring her vision.

The four people at the table she'd served were gaping at her, mouths open, eyes popping.

At least Susie hadn't noticed anything, sitting with her back turned and her legs propped under her, lost in colouring her picture. Kate started towards her, but Mac's deep voice stopped her.

"Better clear off this booth and offer your table over there more coffee," he said. "We usually get a small lunch rush on Tuesday because the mine holds a safety meeting across in the town hall, and the guys come here to eat."

She whirled around and stared up at him.

He was a good six inches taller than her own five eight, long legged, broad shouldered and fit looking. Under his snug white tee, his arms were toned and muscular.

His face was more rugged than handsome, deeply tanned and craggy. He wore a blue stocking cap pulled over dark wavy hair escaping around his ears. He had amazing eyes, deep set, dark almost navy blue with flecks of gold. She'd noticed his eyes when he was talking to Susie.

And he was strong. He'd easily tossed that horrible man out the door.

He tipped his head to the side and raised one thick eyebrow. "You want the job or not, Boots?"

She swallowed hard and nodded. "Yeah. Yeah, I *really* want it." He had no idea how much she needed it. And this town was small and out of the way. Jack Ames wouldn't find them here.

Would he? She shuddered.

"Then snap to it. And come in the kitchen and I'll teach you how to carry out more than one plate at a time."

She tipped up her chin and gave him a mock glare. "*Two* plates. I can carry two at a time." The show of bravado made her feel better.

He blew out a breath and rolled his eyes. "Pathetic. Fours the minimum, Angie does six. And make sure you have all the coffee pots full. You can also set up the big table over by the windows with cups and cutlery, the mine guys like to sit together. Usually about ten of them."

She looked up into his eyes. Her voice trembled a little. "Thank you, Mac. For giving me another chance."

He shrugged. "Floyd's an asshole, this was past due. It was a pleasure to watch you in action." He jerked his chin at the golfers. "See if they want dessert, we've only got what's on the menu, brownies or carrot cake with cream cheese icing."

For the rest of the morning Kate worked hard. Susie grew bored with colouring, and with Mac's permission, Kate ran over to the garage and got the carryall with her daughter's toys from the car.

Susie settled again in the back booth, playing with her collection of plastic horses.

When the noon rush was over, Mac handed two bowls of soup and a plate of sandwiches to Kate.

She recognized number 10 from the menu.

"Take an hour, go have lunch with the kid." He frowned. "Will she eat soup or does she need another smoothie?"

"She should be fine with this. Noodles are her favourite, and she hasn't complained again about her stomach hurting. And I put the tip money the golfing people left in a jar behind the counter."

"Tip money's yours."

"Oh no, I'm only practicing. I wouldn't think of—"

"It's yours. Don't argue. I hate arguing. Voices get loud and it hurts my ears."

"Okay. No arguing. You need another sign." She smiled at him and he nodded. She wasn't certain he got the joke.

Susie devoured the soup and managed half a peanut butter and jam sandwich, chattering all the while about her toy horses.

Kate was touched at Mac's thoughtfulness—he'd made Susie PB&J which definitely went against his prominent sign about substitutions, but her own sandwich was the delicious chicken salad from the menu, and she inhaled it. She'd been too busy to realize how hungry she was.

"Are we gonna stay here in this town, mommy?" Susie's eyes were heavy. "Where is we gonna sleep?"

"At the hotel, right over there." Kate pointed at the building across the street. Hopefully she'd have enough to pay for one night's stay. Mac hadn't indicated whether he intended to pay her or not, but he was feeding them. And he'd insisted about the tips. "I don't know how long we'll stay here, Susie, it depends on the car getting fixed. But I have to work now, so maybe we can make a little nest here in the booth where you can have a nap?"

"You be here all the times if I sleeps?"

"Absolutely. I'd never go away and leave you." Kate smiled at her daughter, but her heart ached at how insecure the past difficult weeks had made the girl. And she'd been sick besides. Her small heart shaped face was pale and her emerald green eyes had dark circles under them.

She simply had to make some money. She couldn't let her daughter sleep in the car, which was possible if the car repairs ate up her remaining cash. She had to find a way to keep them both safe.

The now familiar sense of imminent danger made Kate's heart pound. "Come in the bathroom and we'll wash your hands and face, and then you can have a rest."

She settled Susie with her blanket and pillow, her

favourite toy horse and a kiss, and within moments she was asleep.

Kate did her very best to apply all the things Mac taught her. There were only a handful of customers, so there was time to practice carrying plates and setting up tables.

There was also time to read the long list of rules Mac had posted by the entrance.

NO GUNS
NO HATS—TAKE OFF YOUR HAT!
NO SUBSTITUTIONS
NO DOGS OR OTHER ANIMALS
NO FREE REFILLS EXCEPT ON COFFEE
BREAKFAST ENDS ELEVEN A.M.
NO VEGETARIAN OPTIONS
NO SWEARING. NO RUDE LANGUAGE.
NO NOISE

And a new one he'd added ten minutes ago, the one that she couldn't quite believe.

NO CREDIT CARDS. DEBIT ONLY.

She was no expert on restaurants, but that would surely be a deterrent to anyone coming in to eat. And if there were no customers, she'd be out of a job quick.

Just before his stated closing time of four PM, she went into the kitchen. Mac hadn't ventured out since the scene with Floyd. She eyed the wall of clocks, amazed that every single one showed the exact same time. You'd think that with—how many? She counted twenty-two. You'd think at least one would be a couple minutes out.

"Is there anything you want done in here, Mac? Anything I can help with?"

He was wearing headphones and she had to go and touch his arm to get his attention. She repeated her question.

"No. Thank you." He was emptying the massive dish-washer. He'd taken off the blue stocking cap. His hair was longer than she'd expected. It had been tucked up under the cap and now it curled softly around his ears.

"You're finished for the day, Boots. I don't do dinners, just breakfast and lunch. You planning on coming back to work tomorrow?"

"Yes. Absolutely. I mean as long as you need me here?"

But with no credit cards accepted, he couldn't possibly need her. Even with the cards there were very few customers.

But after a moment he nodded. "Angie's got the flu, probably be out for the rest of the week and most of next. I'd like you to stay at least that long, no point in training you for any less. I close Sunday and Monday, so Tuesday to Saturday. That okay with you?"

She opened her mouth to say something about the credit thing and then closed it again. It was his business.

"Two weeks, then. Of course. What time should I come in the morning?"

"I open at six."

"I'll be here." Lucky thing Susie had always been an early riser.

"Come at five thirty seven, you and the kid can have breakfast before you start."

"I'll pay for the meals." He couldn't afford free meals on top of hiring her.

But he shook his head. "Meals are part of the deal."

She wondered what the deal was. She was just getting up nerve to ask when he pulled a folded wad of money out of his apron pocket and shoved it at her. A glance told her it was far more than she could possibly have earned in one day.

She handed it back at him, shaking her head, but he wouldn't take it.

"It's pay for a couple days work. And the tips, I told you about the tips. You'll keep your word about working."

She swallowed hard. "I absolutely will, I promise you. Thank you." She hoped her relief didn't show on her face.

He nodded and then pointed at her boots. "You and Susie ride horses?"

"Yeah, we do. We *did,*" she corrected herself. "A friend let us ride his horses on weekends. He had a pony Susie loved. Edward was an old friend," she said with a catch in her voice. "He died a week ago. He was eighty three."

Mac shook his head. "Sorry. It's hard when people die."

"Yeah, it really is." Kate sighed. "He was like a grandpa to Susie. She talks about him all the time and wants to know when he's coming back." Edward was probably the closest thing to a grandpa Susie would ever have. Kate's father had walked out on her and her mother when Kate was just three, and they'd never heard from him again.

Her mother had died of cancer ten months ago, and Kate still missed her every moment of every day. Susie was starting to forget, which in a way, was a good thing. At first she'd asked about her Nana a dozen times each day, and they went through the 'Gone to heaven to live with God,' over and over. Susie figured there was no reason she and Kate couldn't visit.

"I have three horses. Maybe you and Susie could come to the farm and ride them. Sometime. When the Truckstop is closed, Sunday or Monday."

She gave him a grateful smile. "We'd love that." She waited for him to say when, but instead he said, "So you're heading off to Vancouver, you know anybody there?"

"My cousin Germaine." She didn't add that Germaine

hadn't exactly been overjoyed when Kate phoned and said she was coming. She'd asked Germaine if she knew of a cheap place to stay while she sorted out a job and a permanent place to live, hoping against hope that Germaine would offer them a bed for at least a day or so.

She didn't. "I'll see what I can do," she'd said. "Not much for rent here in the city. I gotta go, Henry's home from work."

Germaine and Kate had played together as children, as close as sisters. Then Germaine had gotten pregnant and married Henry, the guy she dated in high school, and they moved from Calgary to Vancouver.

Henry and Kate had disliked each other from the beginning, but in spite of everything she and Germaine had stayed friends, emailing and occasionally Face Timing.

But when Kate testified against Ames, Germaine told her tearfully that Henry had warned her not to have anything to do with Kate ever again, that it could be dangerous.

Which was probably true. Jack Ames was a psychopath and a stalker. She shuddered just thinking of him.

Worrying over it all wouldn't help, Kate reminded herself. Besides, she had things that had to be done right now. "Is there a laundromat? Susie was sick in the car, and I need to wash her clothes and the blankets. After I check into the hotel."

"Laundromat's over behind the grocery store." Mac thought for a moment. "There's also a B&B in town, you can phone and ask Blanche if she's got room. It's cheaper than the hotel, lots nicer, and she'd probably let you use the washer and dryer. Tell her you're working for me."

"Does she take kids?"

"Don't see why not. Ask her."

He gave her the number, and within a few moments, she had a place to stay at an amazingly reasonable amount, and the use of the laundry facilities. She gathered Susie and all her things together and tried to put some of the profound gratitude she felt into her voice.

"Thanks so very much for everything, Mac. See you in the morning."

He just nodded and locked the door behind her. He was definitely a man of few words. She thought about all the clocks and his fixation on the exact time, the signs he posted, his aversion to talking to customers.

He had a beautiful voice, deep and resonant, and a slow, measured way of speaking. He didn't smile much, but when he did, it was reflected in his eyes.

He was a strange man, but he was kind. And very attractive. More important, she trusted him, which was weird, because after Ames she hadn't trusted many men at all.

3

Susie clinging to her leg, Kate rang the doorbell of the modest looking two storey grey house a short four blocks from the Truckstop. The front garden was interesting, a collection of shrubs, trees and flowers all mulched with straw, with two live mule deer happily chomping away at a pot of herbs.

"You must be Kate." The older woman smiled and crouched to Susie's height. She had hair like a dandelion gone to seed, an expensive haircut, designer jeans and a figure any woman would envy. Tiny lines around her eyes made Kate think she was maybe in her late forties, but it was hard to guess.

"And this is Miss Susie, how do you do? Come on in, both of you. I'm Blanche Carlson."

"Thanks so much for taking us."

Blanche waved away the thanks. "Anyone Mac vouches for is always welcome. Right this way."

The upstairs room she showed them to was large, bright and well decorated in shades of cream and brown. There were twin beds, a dresser, a soft shaggy rug and a long, low window with a wide padded window seat. A beautiful stand-alone antique closet stood in one corner.

"Bathroom's down the hall, shared with two other rooms, but at the moment you're alone up here. Make yourselves comfortable and then come down and join me for a cup of tea. Laundry's off the kitchen, you can wash your things while we talk." Blanche winked at Susie. "You like lemonade? And some oatmeal cookies?"

Susie nodded vigorously.

Kate had stopped at the garage and gathered from her car what they needed as well as the blanket, clothing and toys that had to be washed. She'd loaded them into two black garbage bags. Then she folded the clean things into the drawer and hung their fresh clothes in the cupboard, leaving the smelly ones in the other bag.

"Is we going to live here now, mommy?"

"*Are* we. And yeah, we'll be here for at least two weeks."

"I likes this bed, mummy." Susie bounced on it and giggled.

"We'll love sleeping here, peanut." She felt safe for the first time in days. She was exhausted, and the other twin looked all too inviting. "Right now, though, lets go down and find the laundry."

"And cookies, mommy. The branch lady said cookies."

Kate smiled and hugged Susie. "*Ms. Blanche*," she corrected. "So she did. Lets go have some before she changes her mind."

Blanche's kitchen smelled of cinnamon and freshly baked cookies, with just a hint of the elusive perfume she wore.

"Come sit down here," she invited Susie, piling cushions on an armchair so the girl could reach the table. She pointed to an adjoining room.

"Right through there, soap is on the shelf.'

"I'll get some and replace yours," Kate said.

"No need. Here's your lemonade, Susie."

"Thank you Mizzz Blanche."

"You have good manners, young lady." Blanche smiled at Susie and waited until Kate was done loading the washer before she sat down.

"So you're working for Mac. And you had a run in with Floyd." Blanche's smile was teasing. "Sounds as if you came out the winner, good for you."

Kate knew her expression reflected her surprise.

Blanche laughed and shook her head. "It's a small town, news spreads like a virus. Now tell me how you happened to start work at The Truckstop?"

Kate quickly explained about the car and added that they were on their way to Vancouver.

"I think Mac was kind of desperate," she added. "Otherwise he'd never have hired me. I've never waitressed before." She paused. "He seems sort of—" she was going to say eccentric, but changed it to, "sort of—shy?"

"Mac loves cooking and hates dealing with people," Blanche said. "You'll get to know him, he's a real sweetheart."

"Is Angie his wife? He mentioned that she had the flu—?"

Blanche shook her head. "Angie's his cousin on his mother's side. He's not married. He had a rough breakup a while back, his fiancee left him for another guy which I figure was a stroke of luck. For Mac. The rumour mill has it that she cleaned out their bank accounts, though."

"Wow." That was something she could really relate to. "Much the same thing happened to me. Well, the same *sort* of thing. I put all my savings into shares of the small energy company I was working for. The CEO disappeared with all the money when the oil market tanked. The company folded, we all got laid off. We lost all our investments and I wasn't able to find another job." And she'd used up a frightening amount of her meagre savings trying to find one.

Which was only part of it, the lesser part. Jack Ames was released from jail the same week she lost her job. And the anonymous phone calls had begun. And then Edward died.

"That's rough." Blanche nodded towards Susie. "What's happening with cutie while you work?"

That was bothering Kate. "Mac said she could hang around the cafe."

Blanche shook her head. "That's no way for a little kid to spend her days. There's a summer program at the library for preschoolers whose parents work, I'm sure Joanne would make space for Susie. Should I call her and find out?"

Kate was hesitant. "She's gotten really clingy with all the changes, I'm not sure."

"Joanne's a marvel with kids, three of the gang at the library are hers and all the other kids love her."

"What do you think, peanut? Would you give it a try?"

"Not leave me, mommy." Susie's tiny chin trembled.

"This would be just like when you stayed with Zoe in Calgary. You loved going to Tiny Tots, remember? I have to go to work, sweetie. It's boring for you to stick around the cafe when you could be having fun with other kids. You know I'll come and get you the moment I'm done. Just like before."

But Susie shook her head and her tiny chin quivered. "I come *wiff* you."

Kate sighed. "Okay Suse. We won't argue about it."

"Maybe Joanne can bring the mountain to Mohammed," Blanche said with a wink at Kate. "I'll give her a call later and explain the situation. Now drink your lemonade, gobble down those cookies, and I'll give you a rundown on Starwood."

Blanche had a wicked sense of humour and for the next half hour she had Kate giggling at her outrageous depiction of the small coal mining town and it's eccentric citizens, never naming anyone, but managing to reveal hilarious and touching vignettes of a small, tight knit and ingrown community.

By the time she took Susie up to bed, Kate felt safer and more relaxed than she had in weeks. No one except her best friend Dana Kramer knew where she was, and Dana wouldn't tell anyone. There was no way Ames could track her to Starwood.

On the throwaway cell she'd bought she tapped out a message to Dana, telling her they were safe.

Then Kate slept deeply and so did Susie.

AT TEN TO six the next morning, Kate tapped on the door of the Truckstop, Susie glued to her leg like velcro.

The closed sign was still in place, but in a few moments Mac opened the door.

"You're late. Sit down," he said gruffly, heading into the kitchen.

Kate hesitated, not knowing whether to sit at a booth or follow him into the back. It didn't look as though he was much of a morning person. And she was only about five minutes late.

"Sit," he called out, and a moment later appeared with a smoothie, an order of eggs and toast and bacon.

"Number 10 on the menu. Without the smoothie."

Kate and Susie slid into a booth and Kate got straight up again to pour coffee into two cups and set up three places. He put the orders down, looking at the second cup of coffee and the extra place setting.

"You'll join us, Mac? I need to know what the specials are." She also needed to let him know the cafe was about to get overrun with little kids, and she was nervous about it. The last thing she wanted to do was cause him enough grief so he'd fire her.

Blanche had tapped on her bedroom door late last evening to ask when she wanted breakfast and tell her that Joanne Logan was bringing all her charges to the cafe to meet Susie early this morning.

Kate had explained about the meals at the Truckstop and then worried about how Mac would react to an influx of little kids. She planned to warn him. She was just trying to figure out how.

Obviously reluctant, Mac sat down, adding cream and sugar to his cup, two precise measures of sugar, one ounce of cream.

"No specials," he said. "Never do specials. Only what's on the menu. No substitutions."

Not very exciting. But maybe Starwood didn't want exciting?

Kate was about to broach the subject of the imminent child invasion when Susie said, "You got Cheerios, Mister Mac?" She'd taken a single tiny sip of her smoothie and wrinkled her nose. "*Pleeeease?*" she added.

"Matter of fact, I do." He grinned across at her. "Between you and me, kiddo, that's my favourite breakfast. But keep it secret, I'm not putting it on the menu."

He went into the kitchen and was back right away with the box, two bowls and a carton of milk. He handed the box to Susie who promptly grinned at him and dumped a mound into her bowl and pushed the cereal across the table.

"Thank you, Mister Mac."

The two of them added milk and then munched noisily.

"Mac, there's something you need to—"

Too late. Banging on the window.

A blonde woman with big red glasses and spiky hair had her smiling face pressed against the glass. She had a baby carrier strapped to her chest. She waved and motioned towards the door.

"It's Joanne, what the heck does she want?" Mac got up, unlocked the front door and opened it.

A horde of small children poured through the door, racing past his legs, yelling and giggling, chasing one another, climbing on the booths and jumping.

"Hi Mac, hope you don't mind I brought the kids," the woman called over the uproar as she slid into the booth across from Kate.

It was obvious Mac minded.

He made a bee-line for the kitchen.

4

———

"You must be Kate, I'm Joanne Logan. And I'll bet this pretty girl is Susie." Joanne's smile was a mile wide, her big hazel eyes behind the huge frames twinkling with good humour. "Hiya Susie. The kids wanted to come and meet you, they love finding a new friend."

Susie huddled against Kate, watching the noisy chaos with wide eyes and then fixing her attention on the baby on Joanne's chest.

"This is Zalika, she's nearly brand new. Come over and have a look?"

Susie hesitated and then ducked down under the booth, popping up like a turtle beside Joanne, who lifted the tiny baby out of the carrier. "Let's clear a space and you can have a closer look at her."

Kate moved the breakfast clutter out of the way.

Joanne unwrapped the baby's blanket.

Enraptured, Susie touched the shock of black hair on the baby's head and then stroked her tiny foot.

"She so *little*," she breathed.

Several other small girls came running over. "She cries when she needs to eat," one said importantly.

"And she goes poo in her diaper," another volunteered and clapped a hand over her mouth to hide her giggle.

"My name is Lizzie, this is my friend Maria. What's your name?" the first one said.

"Susie. Do we gets to hold her?"

"Yup, but only when I'm right here," Joanne said. She bundled the baby up tightly again and put her gently in Susie's arms.

"You gotta support her head," Lizzie instructed.

"You gotta hold on tight cause she wriggles," Maria added.

Susie was barely breathing, cuddling the bundle to her narrow chest. The baby stretched, shooting out a tiny fist that grazed Susie's cheek. She looked up at Kate with huge eyes, her mouth open in amazement. "Her touched me, mommy."

"She," Kate corrected with a lump in her throat. Tony had wanted lots of babies. He'd never even seen his daughter. The accident on the oil-rig had occurred when she was just two months pregnant with Susie. They'd only been married six months.

"I can tell you're really good with babies," Joanne said, keeping a very close eye on things.

"We gots a baby doll over at the libr'y, you feed it and it pees in it's diaper too," Maria announced. "You oughta come and see, we gots a doll house and a stroller and dress up clothes."

"And we gets a story and snacks, right, Joanne?"

"Right. And we'd better make tracks out of here before Mac calls the cops. Besides, Zalika's gonna get hungry any minute and we'll have to feed her. I'll bet you could help me with that, Susie." Joanne took Zalika and gently inserted her back into the chest carrier.

"Come on, come wif us," Maria said, taking Susie's hand and tugging her off the seat. "She makes noises when she eats, and she does big burps and then she poops. Come and see."

Susie hesitated. She looked longingly at the baby and then at Maria, and finally at Kate. "I need to help feed the baby, mommy. You come get me, okay? Right after your work? You promise cross your heart?"

"I promise." Kate could feel tears threatening. "Cross my heart." She was so proud of her daughter's bravery.

Joanne said, "We'll take great care of Susie. There's some forms you'll need to fill in, I'll have them for you when you come to pick her up. And if there's any problem I know where to find you. Here's my cell number."

Within moments, the last child was out the door, Susie staying close to Joanne and still holding Maria's hand.

Mac stuck his head out of the kitchen. "Susie fell for that?"

Kate nodded. "It was the baby that did it."

"Way better for her than hanging around here." He flipped the sign on the door to open. "Too much noise with those kids, though. It's seventeen and a half minutes past opening time, we're late. Okay, Boots, lets get to work."

THE WEEK PASSED QUICKLY. By the time Saturday arrived, Kate had the waitressing thing pretty well down, and keeping busy meant she had less time to worry over her situation.

She was enjoying the job, but it bothered her that there

were so few customers. Mac was an easy boss and a good teacher, but he was anything but chatty. He *was* attractive, far too attractive for her own good.

There was a sort of buzzing awareness whenever he happened to touch her, handing plates over, loading the dishwasher. Once at the end of the day he'd reached out one large finger and shoved her glasses back up on her nose. She'd lost her breath for a moment, and when she looked up into his face, she'd seen the vulnerability in his eyes.

But he *was* eccentric. She'd asked if she could play music on her iphone and his "no" was definite.

"Don't like noise."

"Not even music?"

"Only when there's time to really listen. Don't like background noise."

She quickly got used to his fixation with time, although in some strange way, time seemed suspended for her in spite of all the clocks in the kitchen.

She stopped worrying so much and just lived each moment separately. She had nothing waiting in Vancouver except a desperate search for a job and a place to live. Here, Susie was happy, staying with Blanche was wonderful. And Mac paid her really well for the days she worked, in spite of the lack of business.

That was bothering her, and she had some ideas about how to fix it, but she hadn't dared to suggest them to Mac quite yet.

The potential for The Truckstop was enormous. She'd found out it was the only cafe in town apart from two fast food outlets. It was close to the Big Truck, widely advertised on the highway as "THE WORLD'S BIGGEST TRUCK" and there were plenty of tourists stopping to look at it. They often came over and stepped in the door, but Mac's endless list of rules put a lot of them off, which made for a terrible waste of business. And The Truckstop wasn't really an inviting space.

The food Mac cooked was predictable, never varying from the menu, but always well prepared, the servings generous. The restaurant was shiny clean, the washrooms scrubbed and scrupulous. But there was nothing on the walls except Mac's rules, no greenery, no art, not even memorabilia. No warmth to greet customers when they walked in the door, so more often than not, they turned and left again.

It was a good half hour drive to reach restaurants in neighbouring towns. The Truckstop ought to be doing a landslide business, and Kate figured she knew exactly how to make that happen. She just didn't have the nerve to propose it to her mostly silent, often taciturn boss.

Sunday was her day off, and Blanche invited Kate and Susie for brunch. Over delicious eggs benny and fresh baked croissants, Kate posed the question to Blanche.

"How come more local people don't eat at the Truckstop?"

Blanche poured orange juice for Susie and coffee for both herself and Kate, then seemed to ponder the question.

"Mac makes it tough on the customers, you must have noticed that."

Kate nodded. "All those rules, right?" She cut up Susie's egg and put strawberry jam on her toast. "And now no credit cards." She shook her head.

"No credit cards? That's a new one. That'll put folks off for sure. There's also the fact that Mac doesn't ever change his menu, and I think people get bored with that. Plus he doesn't do any advertising. And he's not exactly sociable."

Blanche's list was all true. Easy fixes, though, except for his personality.

Maybe she could.....Kate put the brakes on the direction her mind was going. The job was totally temporary, she needed to remember that.

"I think I could help. If he'd let me. Which he won't, he's sort of set in his ways." But she couldn't help listing improvements in her head. She dabbed her toast in her eggs. "I don't want to rock the boat. But the way things are I don't see how he can afford to pay a waitress."

"Business is that bad?"

"Probably worse." Kate reached over and smoothed Susie's dark curls, and her daughter smiled at her, her rosebud mouth smeared with egg yolk and jam. "I'm nervous about suggesting anything to Mac. He's pretty diffi-cult when he's mad." She'd seen him with Floyd.

"Mac's more of a gentle giant than a fighter."

Kate nodded. He *was* gentle, but he also had rigid ideas.

"You find a way to convince Mac there's ways he could turn a profit and I think he'd be grateful."

The problem was finding that way.

"Let's take Miss Susie to the Waterpark, I could use some exercise," Blanche suggested. "It's too nice out there for us to stay inside."

It was. The sun shone, the sky was bright blue, a soft breeze kept it from being too hot.

Starwood was well endowed with parks, playgrounds and a huge rec-centre with a swimming pool, all within walking distance of the B&B. Joanne had told her that the coal mining company, Tech, contributed to the amenities.

"It's a company town, there've been coal mines here since the turn of the century," Joanne explained.

Several of Susie's friends from daycare were at the

Waterpark. Without a backward glance, she ran off with them to play.

"She's really happy here," Kate said. "In just a week, she's made friends and gotten over being clingy. She adores Joanne."

"Maybe you should consider staying here. It's a good place for kids to grow up. Lots of young families."

"I have thought of it." Kate watched Susie giggling and splashing in the pool. "But." She hesitated, wondering how much to reveal. "Well, there's a lot to consider."

"You're most welcome to stay with me until you find a place to rent, if that's worrying you. And I know a guy who could help you with that."

"Thanks. You're very kind. We both love staying with you."

"So besides Mac's lack of business, what else is holding you back?"

"I—there's something....."

Kate struggled with how much to reveal to Blanche. She took a deep breath and made a decision. "This has to be totally in confidence. I'm afraid a dangerous man will try to find me."

5

Blanche looked into Kate's eyes. "I can assure you that I'll respect your privacy," she said in a calm tone. "And I've dealt with dangerous men before."

Kate drew in a shuddering breath. "Susie's father died in an accident before she was born. When she was a year old, I got lonely. I joined a web dating service and met this guy. Walter Jenkins, he said his name was."

Blanche nodded and waited.

"I went out on one date with him. An hour into that first date I knew there was something terribly wrong about him. He gave me the creeps. He scared me. We'd met in a restaurant and I knew I had to get away, but if I walked out I had the feeling he'd follow me and make a scene. So I said I was going to the bathroom. I called my friend Dana on my cell and asked her to come and pick me up. I snuck out the back door and into her car, but he was really smart. He followed us and found out where I lived. After that he harassed me, parked outside my apartment, sent creepy emails and filthy letters. I went to the cops but there wasn't much they could do because the info he gave me about himself was all phoney. His name was actually Jack Ames, but I didn't know that. I'd put photos of me and Susie on Facebook, and he—he started telling me what he'd like to do to me. And to her."

Blanche shook her head and looked over at Susie, squealing as she slid down the slide and into the water.

"Sick bastard."

Kate nodded. "And then Ames was arrested. He attacked another woman he'd been stalking and he got caught. I identified him as the one harassing me, and the cops wanted me to go to court and testify against him. I did, and he was sent to jail for two years. But his lawyer got him out three weeks ago on some technicality. And the phone calls started again, hang-ups and threats. Once he came to my door, I called the police but of course by the time they got there he was gone. On top of that, I'd just lost my job, my mother had died, and a good friend had also recently died. I was scared. So I packed up what I could into my car and we left for Vancouver. The only person who knows where I am is Dana, and she won't give out any information without checking with me first. I text her every night and let her know we're okay."

"But you're afraid he'll find you? You're scared of this Ames creature."

"Yeah. I am. Not so much physically, I took a self-defence class and that's helped some. I got a new cell, cancelled Facebook. I feel safe here."

"You'd like to stay here in Starwood?"

"I really would. I don't have anything in Vancouver to go to, no job, nowhere to live. Even in these couple weeks, I've come to like it here. And Susie's happy."

"But you're afraid this creep might find you here in a small town. If you decide to stay, you have to tell Mac what you've just told me."

Kate shook her head, but Blanche insisted.

"He won't tell another living soul. But he needs to know. What if a phone call comes to the Truckstop, a man asking for you? What if this Ames person should walk in one day? Mac needs to know so he can protect you. And himself." Blanche put an arm around Kate's shoulders. "He's a good man, an unusual one. Difficult in some ways, but interesting. And very, very intelligent and artistic. You know that antique closet you admire so much in your room? Mac made that. He's a genius with wood. He reads constantly, he's marvellous with animals. What shows on the surface isn't at all what he's like inside. You have to confide in him and also help him see that there are ways to improve that business."

She was right, Kate knew that. But doing it was a whole other matter.

The truth was she found Mac more than a little disturbing. There was an unspoken intimacy between them. She didn't want to lose that. She didn't want to hurt him in any way, and she was afraid that criticizing the Truckstop would do that.

BACK AT WORK ON TUESDAY, Kate thought of what Blanche had said. She'd thought of little else all night.

The whole thing was a no win for her—if the business failed entirely, she'd have no job. If she made suggestions and Mac got angry and hurt, same result. If she told him about Ames, he'd likely decide he didn't want to be involved and he'd let her go. Lose, lose, lose.

And if she said nothing at all?

She glanced around the empty café. They'd had four

customers all morning, and it was well past noon. The Truckstop was a sinking ship. All she and Mac were doing was re-arranging furniture on the Titanic.

"Mac? How about a coffee? There's something I want to discuss."

She felt shaky and nervous when he came out of the kitchen and slid into the booth across from her. He certainly wasn't one for small talk. She was figuring out how to begin when he blurted, "There's something you ought to know," he said, adding sugar and cream to the cup she'd filled for him and stirring it vigorously.

"Angie isn't coming back anytime soon, her lungs are bad and the doc's told her she needs to take it easy for a long while. I'd like to just hire you full time, but the way things are going, it looks as if I'll have to sell the business. Or just lock the door and walk away, let the bank have it. So I can't promise any future." The look he gave her was sad, and his words melted her heart, but they also firmed up her resolve.

"But we—you—we can fix that," Kate burst out. "I have some ideas about increasing business that I'm sure would make a difference."

He looked wary. "Oh yeah? Like what?"

"Well, to begin with, all these signs." Might as well jump in the deep end. Kate waved a hand at the ever-growing list on the wall.

"What about the signs?" he bristled.

"They're not conducive to business. They put people off, Mac. Customers come to a restaurant for a pleasant, relaxing experience. Those signs make them nervous."

"Yeah, well, without them there's no order. There have to be some rules that let people know what to do, how to act. Order, there has to be order."

"Most people *know* how to act, Mac. They don't appreciate being treated like pre-schoolers."

"Is that it? Is that all?" He was furious, she could see by the tightness of his jaw and the way he wouldn't look at her.

"Nope." She'd started this, she'd damn well finish it. "You should vary the menu. Maybe put up a blackboard with some specials, different ones every day. Try some unusual entrees, make some different desserts. Pies, people love pies. And advertise, Mac. Put ads in the local papers all through the area, Fernie, Coleman, Blairmore. Put a special offer on Facebook, 10% off if they print it and bring it in. Starwood people drive out of town to eat, other people might drive here if it was interesting enough."

She couldn't tell if he was listening to her or not. He was staring over her shoulder, off towards the window, looking like a thundercloud. So she went right on.

"There's all those people who stop to see the Big Truck. Make lunches to go in boxes that look like old fashioned miner's lunch-kits, put a sign up near the truck to advertise them. Make coal miners cookies, coal miner's stew, coal miner's brownies. Pick and shovel pie. Capitalize on the coal miner thing."

"I don't make pies. Chamber won't allow signs." His jaw was set in a stubborn line.

"I don't see why not. It's helping local business. And maybe open a couple days of the week for dinner, everyone likes going out for dinner. You could try, Mac. That's all I'm suggesting, just that you *try* different things. Some may not work, but some will. And business will improve, I know it will." Her heart was pounding. "Mac, I really want this job."

He looked at her with those amazing eyes and she had to swallow hard. Was it *him* she wanted? She heard herself babbling.

"Maybe not forever, the job I mean, I'd like to get back into advertising someday, but for now, working here is good, for me and for Susie. I'd like to stay here in Starwood, find a place we could rent. So finding ways to make the Truckstop profitable benefits me as well as you. Couldn't you just give it a try, Mac? Please?"

She hated sounding as if she was begging, but—what the heck, she was begging.

The atmosphere felt electrically charged, as if lightning was imminent. She braced herself. At least her car was fixed, so she could leave Starwood when he fired her. It had cost her most of what was left of her money, but it would get them to Vancouver.

Her heart hurt for Susie. She was going to miss her new friends, the baby, Joanne.

Her heart hurt for herself. She was going to miss The Truckstop and Blanche. She was going to miss him, this glowering impossible man staring at her across the table.

She hoped he wasn't about to yell at her, she hated being yelled at. But he hated noise, so probably he wouldn't yell.

He was quiet so long it was all she could do to sit and wait.

"Kate, you ever hear of Aspergers Syndrome?"

The abrupt change of subject surprised her so much she had to wonder if he'd heard anything she'd just said. "Yeah, yeah, of course. There've been references to it on the news a couple times, and I saw that movie with Claire Danes about the woman who has it. Temper somebody."

"Temple. Temple Grandin. Yeah, well I have a very mild form of Aspergers. I have this need to control things. I'm socially challenged, I don't play well with others. I tend to be rigid about boundaries, obsessive about things that interest me." A sad smile flitted across his rugged features. "I always knew there was something off about me, I figured I was just stupid. People figured I was weird. It wasn't until a year ago when a doc gave me some tests that I understood what was wrong with me. It was such a huge relief to know what it was. I'm not stupid. I am fairly weird, though. I have Aspergers."

She was so surprised she didn't even know where to begin, so she chose the obvious. "But—then--why on earth would you decide to do something that involves the public if it's hard for you? What made you decide to open a restaurant?"

"I was going to be a woodworker, build furniture, build houses. I love making things out of wood. But then my dad died and my mom got sick and couldn't manage. She refuses to sell the farm, so I came home from trade school to help. Mom and a friend of hers had started the Truckstop eight years ago. It was pretty busy back then. Her friend died and mom inherited it, but she's got early onset Alzheimer's. I needed a job besides just the farm. So I took some cooking classes." He gave that sad grin again. "Cooking suits me, recipes are exact. Like formulas. Like working with wood. Recipes don't keep changing. But nothing in here worked right." He jerked a thumb towards the kitchen. "All the appliances kept breaking down. The roof leaked. The floor had old carpeting, it was dirty. So I took out a bank loan and replaced everything. It had to be right, see. It had to be clean."

Aspergers. It explained so much about him, things that had puzzled her; his rigidity, the refusal to have any music playing, the lists, his attitude towards customers. She didn't know a whole lot about Aspergers, but she'd do some research as soon as she got off work.

Warmth filled her at how open he was, how honest, how

self-aware. Blanche was right, he was an unusual man. She wanted to hug him. She wanted to do more than just hug, but this wasn't the time. She shoved her glasses up her nose. "So will you let me make some changes, Mac? Just to see what happens?"

His inner struggle was evident. Change was tough for him, that was obvious. He rubbed his hands up and down his apron. "What's it going to cost? Because I don't have much money."

She'd figured out a rock bottom price on what was totally necessary. She told him and waited.

"Oh, what the hell," he growled. "Go ahead. Business can't get much worse. Might as well throw what little money there is to the wind." He got up and started towards the kitchen.

"Mac, wait. That's not all."

He waited a moment before he turned around.

"What?" He looked and sounded out of sorts.

"Could you—please, could you sit down again for a minute?" Her voice was shaking.

He slid back into the booth.

"There's this man." She blurted out the whole story that she'd told Joanne, not able to look at him as she spoke. She felt so stupid, so gullible. Heat rose from her chest and crept in a burning tide up over her face as she told him about Ames. It was humiliating to admit that she'd been lonely enough to meet someone on a dating site. It was horrifying to realize how vulnerable she'd made her beloved Susie. And now Mac would be vulnerable too, if Ames ever found her here.

Her voice trembled, and when she was done she felt tears burning. She kept her gaze on the table as they rolled down her cheeks.

She jumped when he laid his hand on hers. She glanced up at him.

"It wasn't your fault. It's not your fault," he repeated in a gentle voice. He handed over several paper napkins and gently removed her glasses.

His usual stern expression was gone. His eyes were filled with sympathy and he took her hand again. "You can't blame yourself, Boots, this guy is obviously a nut case. It's pretty unlikely he'd find you here, but if he does, we'll deal with it. Trust me on that. You don't need to be afraid. Not as long as I'm here."

She was aware of turning her hand palm up, meeting his hand palm to palm.....and of the hot thrill of awareness that shot through her. Her breathing was doing funny things. She couldn't quite see him clearly what with the tears and without her glasses, but she heard him breathing. Same jerky way she was.

And something hard and sore in her seemed to melt away.

6

Just for an instant, Mac thought of getting up and drawing her into his arms. She looked so damned pitiful, so scared. So alone. And touching her was addictive; each time it happened he wanted more. He hated to see her cry.

He drew his hand away. He'd vowed no more women, but vows were made to be broken, that's what Blanche always said.

It was a strange feeling, this thing he felt about her. Most of the time, around mostly anyone, he just wanted gone: either them or him, gone. He didn't like touching people.

He'd liked being close to Brianna. Not just the physical lovemaking, he was really good at that, which was great, but also he'd thought she understood. Why he was the way he was.

Sure, she'd made fun of his obsessive neatness, his attention to detail. He'd hoped after they were married she'd get used to it, and he'd vowed to himself that he'd make a real effort to change. As much as was humanly possible for him.

Instead she'd found someone else. And taken off with Mac's money as well as her new lover.

So keeping his distance from Kate was a good idea. It was just hard because they worked together and a thousand times a day her fingers touched his, her shoulder brushed against him, her vanilla smell filled his nostrils. And each time his libido went into overdrive. And she talked to him, telling him stuff, just like she had just now. She trusted him. He had to keep his distance from her, or he'd get really hurt all over again.

He hurried into the kitchen and started the daily soup.

BUT FOR THE next two weeks, his libido took second place to his temper. He had to do deep breathing to keep from having a total screaming fit, a melt down, over all the changes she made.

First she took all his signs down and put up a wooden one she'd gotten from god knows where. It said, "SIT LONG, TALK MUCH, EAT LOTS." It gave him a sore stomach.

She put plants around the place. Green everywhere. He didn't mind those too much, but she also got a big black-board from somewhere.

She propped it against the wall, but he couldn't stand it messy like that so he screwed it up beside the pass-thru like she wanted, letting her know with angry gestures of the screw driver and sidelong glares what he thought.

And then she started nagging him about making different things that she could mark up as a daily special on the stupid board.

She brought in some old cookbooks from the library, regional ones where locals offered their favorite recipes.

"Maybe just try a couple, Mac. This cheese pie looks like something I'd love to order. And these Cornish hand pies were obviously designed to put in miner's lunch boxes."

And salads, she had a dozen different weird salads she'd found on the internet and printed off for him. "They'll go really well with stuff you're already serving, adding lots of colour. This spinach one is perfect for the hand pies, it'll look so pretty on the plate."

Cranberries. What kind of spinach salad had cranberries?

And somehow, god knows how, she got permission to put up a sign by the Big Truck.

"BIGGEST LITTLE TRUCKSTOP IN THE WORLD"
Come over and try our daily homemade miner's specials and award winning pies. Free dessert for the first twenty customers.

He was stunned when he saw it on his way to work Tuesday morning. When she came through the door at quarter to six he was waiting. He ignored her cheery greeting and roared, "What the hell do you think you're doing, offering free dessert without even asking me? I can't afford to give away dessert. And award winning pies? I've only just started making the damned things, where is the award supposed to be from?" He knew he was shouting but he was too mad to control his voice. And he hated noise, and he hated shouting.

Susie slid behind her mother's legs, peeping out at him with wide, frightened eyes.

He was ashamed for scaring the kid. He was just furious with her mother. He winked at Susie and went to get the box of Cheerios.

"It's called advertising, Mac." Kate didn't seem the least bit afraid of him. He was glad of that. He didn't want her scared of him. He just wanted her to see reason—*his* reason.

"And there's only one free dessert per table. It says so on the bottom of the sign."

He'd been too mad to read the whole stupid thing.

"There'll usually be more customers than one at each table, and when they see the pie they'll all want some. We'll charge for the extras."

She set Susie up at their regular booth and poured coffee for herself and him, orange juice for Susie. She even added the exact right amount of sugar and cream in his cup.

"You *will* win awards for the pies, that one you made yesterday was a total winner. That woman from Tech who stopped in to have lunch said it was to die for. That's an award, if you ask me."

After a couple of dismal failures, he'd gotten a recipe from his mother for pastry, a bulk one that made five double crusts at one time. She'd said it was no fail, and he'd been relieved to find out she was right. But who'd ever heard of putting vinegar and egg in pie-crust?

And then Kate had advertised it as Pick N' Shovel Pie. The stupid name embarrassed him. Even the one on his mom's original recipe was ridiculous, *Flapper Pie.*

"Now, maybe today you could try those Cornish hand pies? We'll advertise it as miner's lunch with the cucumber salad."

"Haven't got any cucumbers."

"I'll zip across and get some when I walk Susie to the library. How many do you need?"

"Two. Nobody'll order hand pies anyhow. Nobody's ever heard of them."

Susie finished her Cheerios and her juice and waved a cheery goodbye when Kate took her to the day care. And as they went out the door he remembered that Kate had somehow gotten him off the subject of the free desserts. She had this way of distracting him.

And then a group of five came in and he had to serve them, which made him anxious and mad at her for not being there to do it.

They ordered the Hungry Miner's Breakfast she'd chalked on the blackboard. Which was really the same thing that used to be number seven on the menu, so making it was the easy part.

And when she hurried back in with a half dozen cucumbers he was too relieved to have her take over the customers to go back to the free dessert thing.

He had an idea about how to show her she was wrong, though. He tripled the recipe for the pastry and made a couple dozen hand pies with hamburger and turnip and potato and carrot, and then he used the leftover pastry to make two banana cream pies and two lemon.

Most of which he'd have to throw out at the end of the day because they'd never have enough customers to eat them all. He could freeze the hand pies but the dessert pies would have to go. He'd make sure Kate saw him chucking out the food, he knew she had a thing about waste. The thought calmed him down. She'd see this new plan of hers wouldn't work. Couldn't work.

He had to keep interrupting the baking to fill breakfast orders, which annoyed him. Finishing each job before he started the next was his pattern, and he seldom varied from it. There'd always been plenty of time to do the lunch prep, but today for some reason The Truckstop had a breakfast rush that extended all through the morning.

She'd taken down the sign that said breakfast was over at ten. She'd marked on the backboard, *TRY OUR ALL DAY*

BREAKFAST. And this is what came of no rules. No order. He fumed and slammed things around.

By the time he finally got all the hand pies and the dessert pies together and baked, it was noon. He'd made noodle soup for lunch the way he always did, but instead of sandwiches from the menu everyone was ordering the damned hand pies Kate had chalked up on the board.

And then having pie for dessert. With ice cream, which was something else he'd never stocked, too much waste. But today they went through the whole two-quart carton of French Vanilla that she'd brought in with the cucumbers.

He'd turned them all into salad just so he could teach her a lesson and throw it all out, but people ate it, all the ice cream, most of the hand pies, and all the damned sweet pies.

"A few people want to know if you plan on selling frozen hand pies so they can use them for lunches. That's a great idea, Mac. We can advertise them and sell by the half dozen." Her face was flushed and her hair sprang up in madcap curls. She had on a short denim skirt that showed a lot of her legs, and a purple top that outlined her breasts

And her mouth, he couldn't stop looking at her mouth. It was sort of puffy, and it was impossible not to imagine kissing that mouth.

And of course there were her boots, she always wore her boots. And now customers who'd heard him calling her Boots had started calling her that too. It burned him up, others calling her by the name he'd invented.

Things had never been so out of control, inside of him as well as out. But he'd never been as busy cooking, and he loved cooking. So that sort of kept the anxiety away a little. He'd found he could easily memorize new recipes, and that took some of the fear out of all the new menu items.

By the time the disturbing week ended on Saturday afternoon, he was exhausted both physically and mentally. Kate was scrubbing the tables as he added up the day's take on the computer and checked it against the cash and credit receipts. He then added the total from the last six days.

"This can't be right," he mumbled. "Kate, come over here. We can't possibly have made this much in one week."

Kate came and stood beside him and he showed her the figures.

"We did it, Mac." She jumped up and down and clapped her hands, eyes huge, cheeks flushed. "We did it! I knew we could do it. Mac, oh Mac, I'm so glad. *Omigod,* I'm so excited. I knew it, I knew we could do it. And next week is going to be even better, I'll bet on it. I put ads in the all the local papers. And I advertised on line, on Starwood Garage Sale."

She threw her arms around him, hugging him tight and squealing, "You'll soon have the *busiest* little Truckstop in the world."

His arms went around her and she became very still. She looked up at him and with no planning at all, he removed her glasses, lowered his head and kissed her. She stood in his embrace without moving for a long moment. He felt her trembling, and then she kissed him back, winding her arms around his neck.

Things got out of hand then and he kissed her neck and her jaw, her ears—she had these nice ears, flat to her head. He trailed kisses down until he met the neckline of her purple tee.

Her skin was soft like the blue silk scarf his sister gave him for his birthday, and when he started to pull the tee shirt up, she stepped back.

"Gosh, Mac. Omigosh." They were both breathing hard. "That was---whoa! We need to slow down here."

He shook his head. "I don't want to slow down. That was good, Kate. I would like to make love with you. I would love to make love with you. I'm very good at it."

He remembered too late that he'd said that before to a woman and she got mad at him because she thought it was arrogant. But that was a long time ago. Would Kate get mad?

"Yeah, me too. And I'm pretty sure you're right, that you're good. I'll have to see if you're right about that." She touched his lips with her finger, gentle and slow, and he drew in a shaky breath.

She smiled at him and it warmed his face like the feeling he got when the sun was shining on it.

He wanted her something awful.

"But I have to go pick up Susie right now, I'm already twenty minutes late."

"OK. You shouldn't be late for Susie. Maybe we can make love tomorrow? You and Susie could come to the farm and we could all go riding and then when Susie and my mother are asleep we could---"

She laughed, but it was a shaky kind of gentle laugh, not the kind that meant she was making fun of him. And she wasn't mad.

"I keep forgetting how literal you are."

He smiled at her. "We're like that, us Aspies. Direct and literal."

"I'm learning."

Her eyes were huge without her glasses. He could drown in her eyes.

"Do you mind how I am, Kate? Not normal?" He felt shy asking her but he had to know. "Weird?"

"Mac." She frowned at him. "There is no normal, we are all just whatever we are." She paused. "I *like* you. I really, really like you." Her face turned pink and she tried to shove her glasses up, forgetting they weren't there. "Just the way you are."

He'd rather she'd said *love you*, but it was probably too soon.

It was a beginning, though.

AFTERWORD

Thank you for choosing a Bobby Hutchinson romance. I hope you enjoyed reading Truckstop, the first in the STAR-WOOD CHRONICLE'S series.

Next is EVERY LITTLE THING

And then BIGGEST LITTLE MUSTACHE

ALSO, I'd love to give you another of the Emergency series, ARE YOU MY DADDY?

If you sign up, you'll get all my news letters telling you what's coming out and what's free or on special. Love to meet you!

I hope you enjoyed Biggest Little Truckstop, the first in a series called STARWOOD CHRONICLES. You can find the second story here:

EVERY LITTLE THING

It begins with a wedding and ends with a romance. What more could you ask of a small town story?

ALSO BY BOBBY HUTCHINSON

HOW NOT TO RUN A B&B

HIS GUARDIAN ANGEL

A LANTERN IN THE WINDOW

SILENT LIGHT, SILENT LOVE

ROSE'S MAIL ORDER BRIDES AND GROOMS

KNIGHTS OF THE NORTH

A LEGAL AFFAIR

Love Medical Romance?

Try these:

THE BABY DOCTOR

PICKING CLOVER

FULL RECOVERY

ARE YOU MY DADDY

DOUBLE JEOPARDY

DRASTIC MEASURES

ABOUT THE AUTHOR

Bobby Hutchinson was born in a small town in interior British Columbia in 1940. Her father was an underground coal miner, her mother a housewife, and both were storytellers. Learning to read was the most significant event in her early life.

She married young and had three sons. Her middle son was deaf, and he taught her patience. She divorced and worked at various odd jobs, directing traffic around construction sites, day caring challenged children, selling fabric by the pound at a remnant store.

She mortgaged her house and bought the store, took her sewing machine to work, and began to sew a dress a day. The dresses sold. The fabric didn't, so she hired four seamstresses and turned the store into a handmade clothing boutique.

After twelve successful years, she sold the business and decided to run a marathon. Training was a huge bore, so she made up a story as she ran, about Pheiddipedes, the first marathoner. She copied it down and sent it to the Chatelaine short story contest, won first prize, finished the Vancouver marathon, and became a writer. It was a hell of a lot easier than running.

She married again and divorced again, writing all the while, mostly romances, (which she obviously needs to learn a lot about,) and now has more than fifty-five published books.

She's currently working on three or four or eight more books. She has six enchanting grandchildren. She lives alone, apart from two rabbits, meditates, bikes, walks, reads incessantly, and writes compulsively.

She likes a quote by Dolly Parton: "Decide who you are, and then do it on purpose."

www.ingramcontent.com/pod-product-compliance
Lightning Source LLC
Chambersburg PA
CBHW051314160726
47994CB00003B/1452